For: Mom and Dad with love
—D. P.

To my Dad and Mum, who I can never thank enough for their great love
—Z. C.

MELA
and the
ELEPHANT

Dow Phumiruk

and illustrated by Ziyue Chen

PUBLISHED BY SLEEPING BEAR PRESS

Mela set out to explore the banks of the Ping River near her home.
Her little brother followed to the edge of the yard, hoping she'd take him along.

"What will you give me if I take you?"

He had nothing to offer. "Then you stay home," Mela announced.

She turned and skipped along the road and across the grassy field before reaching the steep riverbank. She watched the water sparkle and splash below. Mela hurried down to the river's edge. When she reached the dock, she saw a large fish swimming by.

"What a fine dinner that fish would make!" Mela thought. She
hopped into her uncle's boat, grabbed his net, and tossed it far
into the river to scoop up the silvery fish. But moments later,
she was drifting swiftly downstream.

The current was too strong to paddle back and, before she knew it, Mela was swept deep into the dense jungle.

After a long while,
the boat caught against a
tangle of tree roots.

Mela stepped out onto
a large rock.

She craned her neck to look
back up the river. She was a
long way from home.

A crocodile appeared along the shore. "Crocodile, will
you help me get home? I'll tie a rope to your tail, and
you can tow my boat back upstream."

"What will you give me for my help?" he asked.

"You can have this fish I caught."

The crocodile agreed. But when Mela tossed him the
fish, he snapped it up and swam away.

"Wait!" she called after the crocodile, but he had
disappeared under the water.

Mela looked around her. Tall trees blocked out most of the sun's light. Leaves stirred overhead and the river rushed at her side. She pointed herself upstream and started to walk.

A leopard slinked into sight.
"Leopard, I am lost.
Do you know a way back to the village?"

"I do. What will you give me if I show you?"
Mela thought a moment.
"You can have my sweater. It will keep your cubs warm on cool nights."

Mela held her sweater out for the leopard to see.
But the leopard snatched it up and leaped away.

"How foolish of me," she said, and sighed. She walked on and found a narrow path—soon she was surrounded by towering trees wrapped with ropy vines.

Three monkeys dangled overhead.

"Monkeys! Can you show me a way through the trees and back to my village?"

"What will you give us if we help you?" one chattered.

Mela held out her backpack. "You can have this pack to carry fruit as you travel through the jungle." But the biggest monkey grabbed it from her, and they all swung away.

Mela slumped to the ground and began to cry. Night was falling and soon darkness would settle over the jungle. She shivered. How would she get home now?

Soon, she heard the rustling and snapping of branches.
An elephant lumbered his way toward her.

"Child, are you lost?" the elephant asked.
"I will give you a ride to the village."
   Mela cried even harder. "But I have nothing
left to offer you!"
   "It would make my heart happy
to help you," the elephant said.
"I don't need anything in return."

He lowered his trunk for Mela to climb
onto his great, warm back and he carried
her all the way to the village.

Mela slid from the elephant's back, grateful to be home.
She pressed her palms together in thanks and felt the elephant's
strong trunk embrace her. "Thank you," she said.

The next morning, Mela's brother asked to see the riverbank
where her adventure had begun.

"I'll take you," she said, and together they set off to explore.

Mela remembered what the elephant had taught her:

kindness needs no reward, for it brings happiness and warmth to the heart.

From then on, she offered many
kindnesses to others, asking nothing in return.

AUTHOR'S NOTE *about* THAILAND

This story is set in Thailand, a fascinating country in Southeast Asia. Thailand is famous for its great natural beauty, from beaches with clear blue water in the south to tall green mountains and jungles in the north. The climate is generally hot, with a rainy season from May to October. About 67 million people live in this country, and its nickname is the "Land of Smiles." Did you know that Thailand has a royal family and a Grand Palace in the capital city of Bangkok?

The Ping River in Mela's story is found in northern Thailand. It flows into the Chao Phraya River, a major river that runs through Bangkok. Though Mela's story is set in a rural village, Thailand is not all rural. If you visited Bangkok, you'd probably be very surprised at how modern its downtown is! There are plenty of tall buildings and traffic, just like you would see in any large city.

One particular Thai custom depicted in Mela's story is how we show gratitude. Thai people say thank you by holding their hands together as in prayer and bowing slightly. If you are very, very grateful, or if the person being thanked is much older than you, you will take a much deeper bow. Practice thanking a friend. How would you thank a grandparent? Thai people also put their hands together and bow this way when saying hello or good-bye.

In the story, Mela learns that kindness needs no reward. There is a Thai saying, "Place gold on Buddha's back." Most Thai people practice the religion of Buddhism, and one way they pay respects at temple is to apply a slip of gold leaf onto the Buddha statue (the statues become impressively gilded by loyal Buddhists over time). The saying means that one should perform this act of worship behind the statue, drawing no attention to the good deed. Similarly, a gesture of kindness needs no attention drawn to it.

As Mela learned, being kind to someone makes you feel happy. There are many ways to be kind every day. You can draw a picture for a friend, help with chores around the house, or tell someone that you care about them. I hope you'll remember to be kind to the people you meet every day.